hmhco.com
curiousgeorge.com

The text of this book is set in Garamond.

ISBN: 978-1-328-97311-5

Printed in China
SCP 10 9 8 7 6 5 4 3 2 1
4500748834

Margret & H. A. Rey's

Curious George
Goes Swimming

Written by Alessandra Preziosi

Illustrated in the style of H. A. Rey by Mary O'Keefe Your

HOUGHTON MIFFLIN HARCOURT
Boston   New York

This is George. He was a good little monkey and always very curious. Today, the man with the yellow hat was taking George to the town pool.

It was a hot summer day. There were lots of people at the pool.

George's friend found some empty chairs for them and put their things down. "I'll go find you a float, George," the man said. "Now be a good little monkey."

George sat on the chair and looked around. He saw little kids tossing a beach ball in the shallow end and big kids lined up at the diving board. George couldn't wait to get in the water.

Then he saw a tall white chair with an umbrella—and a red float hanging on it. The woman in the chair wasn't using it. Maybe George could borrow that one.

Like only a monkey could,
George swung up to the top of
the chair and grabbed the float.

But just as he was about to climb down, the woman in the chair turned around. "Hey! You can't take that! That's the lifeguard float!"

She did not sound happy. George let go of the float, jumped back down to the ground, and started running.

Then he heard a whistle
and a loud voice call,
"NO RUNNING BY THE POOL!"

George slid to a stop.

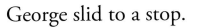

He walked v-e-e-e-e-ry slowly
back to his own chair.

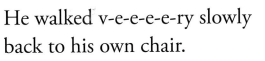

The man was there waiting for him.
"You have to be careful at the pool, George," the man said.
"The ground gets wet and slippery, and you could fall."
George nodded.

Then the man handed George a small foam board. "I got you a kickboard.
You hold on to it in the water to help you float. Why don't you go for a swim?"

George thought that was a great idea. He took the kickboard and got into the pool. The water was cool and refreshing!

Everywhere George looked, kids were having fun. Some were doing swim races across the pool. Some were playing water tag.

Others were even doing handstands in the water!

Then George noticed one little girl holding on to the side of the pool.
George waved for her to come swim, but she wouldn't let go of the edge.

George wanted to show her how much fun swimming was!
He kicked his legs. He paddled his arms. He hopped up on
top of the kickboard like he was surfing.

Surfing would be even more fun if there were waves to ride.
George was curious. Could he make waves with his kickboard?

He pushed the board through the
water and made a small wave.
What fun! George did it again,
pushing a little harder.

That made a bigger wave. George heard
the little girl giggle. She was still holding
on, but at least now she was smiling!

George pushed the board out into
the water as hard as he could and
made a wave so big that—oh no!—
it splashed over the side of the pool!

TWEET-TWEET! He heard the loud whistle again. "No splashing!"

Oops! George hadn't meant to break another pool rule. He swam over to the side and sat down.

Then he saw the little girl pulling herself over to him along the side of the pool. "Hi, I'm Lucy," she said. "I know you didn't mean to splash. It was just an accident. You're a really good swimmer!" George smiled.

"I wish I were a good swimmer like you. My dad has been teaching me. He says I can do it, but I'm scared to let go. I don't like to put my head underwater."

George was curious.
How could he show Lucy how fun a day at the pool could be?

Then George had an idea. Ice cream was a special pool day treat!
The man had put some money for a treat in their bag. He pointed
to the snack bar and then hurried over—very carefully.

In a few minutes, he was back with two ice cream pops—one for him and one for Lucy. "Thank you, George!" She smiled and climbed out of the water. They sat down on the side of the pool to eat their treats.

Just as George was taking his first lick,
the loud whistle blew again!
"NO FOOD BY THE POOL!"
the lifeguard yelled.

George was startled.
He dropped his ice
cream into the pool!

Oh no! It was sinking to the bottom. He had to get it before it made a huge mess. George jumped right in after it.

He swam down to the bottom of the pool—but where was his ice cream?

When he came back up for a breath he saw Lucy— under the water! And she was getting his ice cream!

In a moment, the lifeguard was
there, ready to rescue—but
then Lucy popped back up!

She handed George his ice cream
pop (or what was left of it), and
wiped her hair from her face.

The lifeguard was about to scold them when Lucy broke into a huge smile.
"I did it, George! I swam underwater! And it's all thanks to you!"
This made the lifeguard smile, too. She wrapped them in dry towels
and helped clean up the mess.

It was a great day at the pool.
George had a new friend—and a new ice cream!